AN INDIAN GIVER

AN INDIAN GIVER

A COMEDY

W. D. Howells

GYAN

Published by

GYAN

Gyan Publishing House
5, Ansari Road
Daryaganj, New Delhi-110002
Phone: 011-47034999, 9811692060
E-mail: books@gyanbooks.com

Distribution Network
gyanbooks.com
India, USA, Canada, UK, Australia, France

ISBN: 978-81-212-9075-3 (PB)
First Published, 1900

2nd Impression 2023

Printed at: Gyan Press, Delhi.

AN INDIAN GIVER
AUTHOR: W. D. Howells

An Indian Giver

A COMEDY

By W. D. Howells

BOSTON AND NEW YORK
Houghton, Mifflin and Company MDCCCC

An Indian Giver

A COMEDY

I

MRS. LILLIAN INGLEHART AND MISS ROBERTA LAWRENCE

Mrs. Inglehart: "My dear! I will not hear another word. He is *yours!* The idea of making such a fuss about a little thing like the gift of a young man!"

Miss Lawrence: "It's only that I was afraid you might want him yourself, Mrs. Inglehart. It would make me unhappy if I thought you had deprived yourself of a cousin you might regret. They don't grow on every bush, I believe."

Mrs. Inglehart: "Such as Jim don't, I'll admit. But I hope I know the duties of a hostess, and the first of them is to get a young lady visitor engaged if possible. You've never seen Jim, have you?"

Miss Lawrence: "Never. What's he like?"

Mrs. Inglehart: "Are you very fond of tall men?"

Miss Lawrence: "Is he tall?"

Mrs. Inglehart: "Not so very. I should say he had more breadth and thickness than length."

Miss Lawrence: "Oh, I like them broad and thick."

Mrs. Inglehart: "Do you?" She speaks with a certain intonation of misgiving, and then she has the effect of pulling herself together: "Do you like them brown-complexioned and dark-eyed?"

Miss Lawrence: "Is *he* brown-complexioned and dark-eyed?"

Mrs. Inglehart: "He 's brown-complexioned and blue-eyed."

Miss Lawrence: "Oh, that sort of contradiction is adorable. The blue eyes always have such a funny look in the dark face. I shall like him, I know. When 's he coming?"

Mrs. Inglehart: "Any moment, now."

Miss Lawrence: "Oh!" She jumps to her feet. Mrs. Inglehart remains seated, but leans forward to look in through the door at the clock in the hall, from the veranda where, with a pretense of sewing in her lap, she is talking with her guest. To the right of this hall the windows of a wide drawing-room open to the floor, and people come and go through them as if they were doors. From the veranda, which extends around three sides of the house, broad steps descend to a driveway curving in front of it. Beyond the road green lawns, wept over by drooping white birches, slope to the red rocks that keep Mrs. Inglehart's place from the sea.

Mrs. Inglehart: "Or not *moment*, exactly. He promised to be here by the half past four, but he probably won't come till the five-ten; it's only four now."

Miss Lawrence: "Time enough to prink, then." She sinks back into her chair, provisionally. "Is Mr. Fairford punctilious about prinking?"

Mrs. Inglehart: "I see you would dread that."

Miss Lawrence: "I don't know that I should. They have to have *some* fault."

Mrs. Inglehart: "And you think that is a fault?"

Miss Lawrence: "I can't say that I do. Do you?"

Mrs. Inglehart, with an air of great candor: "To tell you the truth, I don't believe Jim cares about women's dress."

Miss Lawrence: "Then he is the

most dangerous kind. He 'll not see anything, but he 'll feel everything. I shall have to dress at his nerves."

Mrs. Inglehart: "It 's clear that you 've made your observations, my dear."

Miss Lawrence: "By twenty-six, one has."

Mrs. Inglehart: "I should never have dreamt twenty-six."

Miss Lawrence: "I have n't dreamt it myself. In my dreams I 'm still sixteen. It 's only in my waking moments that I 'm twenty-six."

Mrs. Inglehart, thoughtfully: "You have courage."

Miss Lawrence: "I have conviction. It 's best to be honest — unless the man prefers lies."

Mrs. Inglehart: "Don't they all?"

Miss Lawrence: "Nearly all. But if Mr. Fairford should happen to be the exception that does n't, will you please tell him I *owned* to twenty-six, but you don't *know* how much older I really am?"

Mrs. Inglehart, with open admiration and covert alarm: "You 're a strange girl!"

Miss Lawrence: "Will that scare him? Should you advise me to be less strange?"

Mrs. Inglehart, with a sigh: "No; he will like you so."

Miss Lawrence, laughing: "What despair! Poor Mrs. Inglehart! You 're sorry already you gave him to me! Well, you may have him back."

Mrs. Inglehart, with noble constancy: "No, no; you 're the very one for him."

Miss Lawrence: "Then our only hope is that he is n't the one for me."

Mrs. Inglehart: "You think I 'm not in earnest. Well, then, the only thing left is to convince you by practical" —

Miss Lawrence: "Demonstration? I don't see how it can be done. You can't pass this young man along to me without consulting his inclinations. Has he very decided inclinations?"

Mrs. Inglehart: "Yes, he has. That was the trouble, I suppose."

Miss Lawrence: "So there *was* trouble." She smiles intelligently.

Mrs. Inglehart: "It was a great while ago. It was before I was — there was any — Mrs. Inglehart. And there would be the same trouble again, if I were not — there were not any — Mrs. Inglehart. So it 's best to have it over before it begins."

Miss Lawrence: "I see what you mean. He 's one of those terrible creatures who know their own minds; or think they do; and — may I be a little critical of your gift? I know it seems ungracious!"

Mrs. Inglehart: "Not in the least. People change their wedding-presents, even."

Miss Lawrence: "I should n't wish to change the present; only the name: Jim! If it were only Jack, now, I should know what to do. The Jacks are all alike. They smoke, they flirt desperately, but they are very warm-hearted, and conceal a great deal of sentiment under the mask of cynicism — like Thackeray's men. They would do anything for you — at least any little thing like jumping overboard from a yacht to fish your hat up, or marrying a girl that you 've found out is in love with them, and you think they ought, though you 're dying for them yourself. You can twist them round your fingers; but it must be different with Jims. Jim! It suggests something rather grim; perhaps it 's because it rhymes with it. Jim! I should say one's little arts, one's little airs and graces, would be thrown away on Jim. He sounds like a person of convictions: he sounds like a person of opinions, too, and very stiff ones. I suspect that Jim is serious, and he likes seriousness in women. He has ideas of home and a wife, and of being master in his own house. All that could be easily taken out of him if he were Jack, of course; but being Jim, it could n't. He 's masterful; I feel that he 's masterful. He has all sorts of preconceived notions. He would be very domestic, and intellectual, and he would rather read to you than talk to you. He would want to respect you, and if you would n't let him, he would — make it hot for you. Yes, I know the type: adoring, domineering, devoted, and utterly intolerable."

Mrs. Inglehart, who has been leaning forward more and more, and edging almost out of her chair, in her intentness:

"You 've met him! You know him! You 've been letting me give myself away!"

Miss Lawrence: "Mr. Fairford? You? I? You 've given *him* away, but not yourself, at least to me, Mrs. Inglehart. I never saw Mr. Fairford in my life. I never heard of him till I came here."

Mrs. Inglehart: "Then I don't know but it 's worse, for you 've guessed him. How you must dread the idea of him!"

Miss Lawrence, thoughtfully: "I don't know. I rather like the notion of grappling with such a — problem. It would be fun to get the better of it."

Mrs. Inglehart: "And if you got the worse?"

Miss Lawrence: "I don't believe I

should get the worse. But now, really, had n't I better go and prink, Mrs. Inglehart? I don't believe Jim would like to find me unprepared."

Mrs. Inglehart: "No. Go and prink."

Miss Lawrence, going in through the open door: "If he should happen to come before I get down, I know I can trust him with you, Mrs. Inglehart." She vanishes, with a smile over her shoulder at Mrs. Inglehart, who remains silent and motionless, apparently insensible of her withdrawal, though she keeps a mechanical smile of parting on her face. Her mother enters from the door that Miss Lawrence has passed through.

An Indian Giver

II

MRS. WENHAM, MRS. INGLEHART

Mrs. Wenham: "When do you expect James, Lilly?"

Mrs. Inglehart, with a deep sigh: "Oh, any time, now. He said he would be here at half past four."

Mrs. Wenham: "Then he'll *be* here at half past four."

Mrs. Inglehart: "Yes, I suppose he will, — with his tiresome punctuality."

Mrs. Wenham: "Tiresome? If there is one thing more than another that I like in James Fairford, it *is* his punctuality. It's something that I can thoroughly sympathize with him in. If it had not been for *my* habits of punctuality, where would you have been at this moment, Lillian?"

Mrs. Inglehart: "Perhaps not born. But now don't preach, mother. Advise. You'll like it almost as well."

Mrs. Wenham, looking doubtful, but as if assenting for argument's sake: "Well?"

Mrs. Inglehart: "What do you think of Miss Lawrence?"

Mrs. Wenham: "What do you mean by thinking? If you've been behaving foolishly in any way, and want me to help you out of it by blaming Miss Lawrence" —

Mrs. Inglehart: "Blame? Who's talking of blame? I simply wish to know if you don't think she's something of a cat."

Mrs. Wenham: "Cat? How, cat?"

Mrs. Inglehart: "I mean very purring, and sly, and velvety."

Mrs. Wenham: "No, not at all."

Mrs. Inglehart: "Well, then, very sharp and clawy."

Mrs. Wenham: "What have you been doing, Lillian?"

Mrs. Inglehart: "Nothing. I 've been *un*doing. How do you think she and Jim will like each other?"

Mrs. Wenham: "What difference how they like each other?"

Mrs. Inglehart: "One does n't want one's guests to be at sword's points."

Mrs. Wenham: "I don't know why you asked her when you knew he was coming."

Mrs. Inglehart: "I 'm sure they 'll

like each other. He 'll respect her. I respect her myself. She has a great deal of character, and all that; but I think there 's a vein of coarseness in her. Yes, she *is* coarse. She has a bold way of talking about men. It may be very modern, and the rest of it, but I don't like it, and I don't think it 's nicc."

Mrs. Wenham: "What men has she been talking about?"

Mrs. Inglehart: "Oh, — none."

Mrs. Wenham: "What has she been saying about them?"

Mrs. Inglehart: "Oh, — nothing. But girls seem to say anything, nowadays. Especially old ones! How old am I, mother?"

Mrs. Wenham: "You 're twenty-seven. You know that well enough."

Mrs. Inglehart: "And she 's twenty-six, and looks every day of it." Vaguely, after a moment: "I 'm sure *I* don't know how I came to ask her here."

Mrs. Wenham: "Why do you say that, *now?* Have you been making a fool of yourself, Lilly?"

Mrs. Inglehart: "I *won't* be scolded in my own house, mother!"

Mrs. Wenham: "Very well, if you call it scolding." Mrs. Wenham sits very erect in her chair, and gathers all her dignity about her; Mrs. Inglehart rocks to and fro in a reckless and distraught manner. "May I ask a simple question?"

Mrs. Inglehart: "I suppose so."

Mrs. Wenham: "Are you going to accept James?"

Mrs. Inglehart: "What an idea! No!"

Mrs. Wenham: "Then, if it is n't scolding, allow me to say that he will have a right to feel trifled with. Your letting him come here, after what 's past, is tantamount to your saying you would marry him if he asked you" —

Mrs. Inglehart: "Very well, I 'll keep him from asking me, then. There are ways of staving men off."

Mrs. Wenham: "Not such men as James Langton Fairford. You have n't forgotten how he behaved when you tried it before — before your marriage."

Mrs. Inglehart: "That was a great

while ago. I considered him a mere boy, and he might have known it."

Mrs. Wenham: "He was two years older than you."

Mrs. Inglehart: "And how old was I, pray? Nineteen! A perfect chit! That proves that he was a boy. And he was very rude. If he had been a little more — thoughtful, and patient! You know how it was, mother. After Jim's outrageous conduct, I had no alternative but to marry Mr. Inglehart; and I am not going to have it said, now, after all I've been through on his account, that I was in love with him all along, and married him the minute I decently could. I trust I have too much regard for Mr. Inglehart's memory for *that.*"

Mrs. Wenham: "Then allow me to say, my dear, without scolding, that I don't know what you 're after."

Mrs. Inglehart: "I 'm not after anything, if you prefer such a common expression. 'It 's Jim that 's after me; and I shall not feel in the least bound to be overtaken. I have other plans for him."

Mrs. Wenham: "Other plans?"

Mrs. Inglehart: "He may fancy Roberta Lawrence. I 'm sure I don't see what men find in her, all of them. But if it 's frankness, as they call it, I wish them joy of it. Of all the detestable hypocrites in *this* world commend me to a frank woman. Why, it 's nothing but mask upon mask, all the way through!"

Mrs. Wenham: "Is this why you are so down upon the poor girl?"

Mrs. Inglehart: "Down upon her? Well, yes; it may be hate to throw such a husband as Jim Fairford in her way. At any rate I've set my heart upon making a match between them. That will let me out and it will be such fun." She expresses her exultation in rather a lugubrious note of laughter, and tries to escape the severe gaze which her mother fixes upon her.

Mrs. Wenham: "Just one word, Lillian Inglehart! Does Miss Lawrence know anything of this fine scheme?"

Mrs. Inglehart: "No. That is, I have put it out of my power to accept Jim Fairford by telling Roberta Lawrence she may have him if she can get him. If she does, or can, that 's the end of it; and it's the end of it anyway."

Mrs. Wenham: "Well, Lillian, if you are in earnest in what you say, you are certainly the greatest fool — But perhaps you consider this scolding?"

Mrs. Inglehart: "Not at all. I call it reasoning. Go on."

Mrs. Wenham: "Oh, I've nothing more to say. But if you have really told the girl — if you have put this idea into her head, you have done a wrong and wicked thing, and you 'll have to answer for the consequences. It would be no more than you deserve if James *did* take a fancy to her, and I hope he will; and if you have a spark of generosity in your composition, you at least won't try to prejudice him against her."

Mrs. Inglehart: "You have such a low opinion of me, mother, that I wonder you associate with me at all. But now I 'm going to wring your bosom by an act of the most exemplary magnanimity you ever heard of. A splendid idea has just occurred to me. I 'm going to send Roberta down to see Jim first and receive him. She 's upstairs now, prinking, and I 'm going straight to my room, and I 'm going to be so slow getting ready that she 'll have to go down, and she can have him all to herself for a first impression; and a girl of twenty-six knows how to make hay while the sun shines. *Now* what do you say?"

Mrs. Wenham, going in: "Humph!"

Mrs. Inglehart: "You don't believe I'll do it?"

Mrs. Wenham: "I *know* you won't."

Mrs. Inglehart, calling after her: "Well, I'm so glad you approve of the idea, mother. I only wish you could see how expressive your back looks, as you disappear in the distance. It's everything that's appreciative and flattering." As Mrs. Wenham vanishes: "Well, I don't care." In the course of her two dialogues a great many sewing materials and appliances have dropped about Mrs. Inglehart on the floor; as she now rises, her scissors fall out of her lap, and as she stoops to pick them up she is reminded of the other things. "What a bother!" When she has got them all in her lap again, she turns to the door, but is arrested by the sound of a quick, decided footfall on the steps of the veranda. She looks round over her shoulder, and in this very pretty and engaging attitude she meets the blue eyes flashing out of the brown face of James Fairford. He has a robust hand-bag in one hand and an umbrella in the other; over his arm hangs a light overcoat. He is dressed in summer stuffs, but in no concession to the negligence of summer fashion; his shirt is white; his firm legs are cased in trousers that descend to his black shoes; his whole keeping is that of a man who despises the appearance of recreation, and puts business before pleasure. "James!" Mrs. Inglehart's exclamation expresses mingled pleasure, surprise, and dismay. She drops all the things out of her lap again. "What are you doing here at this unearthly hour? You said you would be here at half past four!" She sinks back into her chair.

III

FAIRFORD AND MRS. INGLEHART, WITH MOMENTS OF MISS LAWRENCE

Fairford: "It's half past four now." He sits heavily down in one of the veranda chairs, plants his bag before him, and then pushes it away with his foot, while he mops his forehead with his handkerchief.

Mrs. Inglehart: "Did you walk?"

Fairford: "Do I seem to have driven? And in what?"

Mrs. Inglehart, hiding a smile with her hand: "I wonder how you found the way."

Fairford: "They told me at the station."

Mrs. Inglehart, gracefully sinking into a chair: "Did they tell you that if it had n't been for your ridiculous punctuality you 'd have been met at the train? Now you see what comes of being on time!"

Fairford: "I dare say they would if they could have spared a moment from the celebration of your charms and virtues. You seem to have cast your confounded glamour over the neighborhood, as usual."

Mrs. Inglehart: "Yes, it 's new to me. It must have been the telegraph girl!"

Fairford: "There was a girl, and there was a telegraph. I didn't see them in combination."

Mrs. Inglehart: "They were one, all the same. Yes, I may say she 's quite an ardent admirer."

Fairford: "So am I, Lillian."

Mrs. Inglehart: "Oh yes. But you must n't say it. I hope you were n't rude to the poor girl on that account?"

Fairford: "Why must n't I say it? I 've come here to say it!"

Mrs. Inglehart, to gain time: "But you 've said it before — and you ought to be a little more diversified in your remarks."

Fairford, getting to his feet: "Lillian, how can you trifle with me so? Surely you know what I must understand —

must hope — from your allowing me to come here to-day?" He starts toward her and stumbles over his bag; he kicks the bag: Mrs. Inglehart laughs. "Oh, laugh at me, make a fool of me!"

Mrs. Inglehart: "You know you don't approve of me, Jim; you know you don't."

Fairford: "I believe you can make me approve of you if you choose. And if you don't choose, I want you anyway."

Mrs. Inglehart: "Oh! Do you think that's very logical?"

Fairford, bitterly: "No, I'm not proud of it. As you say, it isn't logical; it isn't reasonable; but I always wanted you; I wanted you long ago, before you were married."

An Indian Giver

Mrs. Inglehart: "Why do people say you don't know how to flatter? I'm sure it's enough to turn *my* poor head to have a man say he isn't proud of caring for me, but he keeps on doing it regardless of consequences."

Fairford: "You know what I mean. I never pretended that you were my ideal in character, but"—

Mrs. Inglehart: "I thought it was customary to tell the lady that she *was* your ideal. That's what they always tell *me!*"

Fairford: "I don't care what other people tell you. *I* tell you the truth; and I tell you that you are *not* my ideal."

Mrs. Inglehart: "What am I, then, if I'm not your ideal?"

Fairford: "You 're — you 're my love. But you know that."

Mrs. Inglehart: "I 've heard you say so. But I 'm not sure that I know it."

Fairford: "Not sure!"

Mrs. Inglehart: "You may not be sure of your own mind."

Fairford: "This is trifling, Lillian. What do you say to me?"

Mrs. Inglehart: "What can I say till I 'm convinced you 're in earnest?"

Fairford: "And what will convince you? It seems to me that it 's proof enough of my sincerity that I 'm here to offer myself to you and to ask you to be my wife. Did n't you know that I was coming to do that? What else do you expect? Do you want me to say that you *are* my ideal, that you are everything in nature and character that I have dreamed of, and that I would not have you different?"

Mrs. Inglehart: "You might try it. I don't know what effect it would have."

Fairford: "You wish me to minister to your vanity, to fill your head with nonsense. Well, I will never do it!"

Mrs. Inglehart: "Then I don't see how it's going to end. You might at least say you believe I could *become* your ideal."

Fairford: "But if I don't believe you could, and therefore I renounce my ideal; if I throw it away, and I tell you that you, whatever you are, are a thousand times dearer than anything I've ever imagined? And yet you might be all that I 've ever dreamed of in woman, prompt, energetic, constant in purpose, with a high sense of duty, a devotion to noble " —

Mrs. Inglehart : " Another James Fairford. What egotism ! Yes, I could easily be all that, if I wanted to. The trouble is I could n't want to."

Fairford : "I know it, and I don't ask it of you. I ask you merely to be yourself, — and to be mine."

Mrs. Inglehart : " Do you think that 's so little, that you say *merely?* Asking a woman to be herself and to be yours is asking everything."

Fairford : " Then don't be yourself ; don't be anything but mine."

Mrs. Inglehart : "Now you are beginning to talk sense " —

Fairford, starting toward her: "And you consent — you" — A sound as of a lifting window above the veranda roof is heard, and then, after a moment, the voice of Miss Roberta Lawrence.

Miss Lawrence: "Mrs. Inglehart!"

Mrs. Inglehart, in a low key to Fairford: "Oh, good gracious, I forgot all about her! *Now* what am I to do?" In a high key to Miss Lawrence: "Yes?"

Miss Lawrence, with a nervous laugh: "Oh, it *is* you. I thought, I was n't sure it was you I heard. What time is it, please?"

Mrs. Inglehart: "It 's a little after four — a quarter — twenty minutes" —

Miss Lawrence: "Then there 's time,

yet." There is a sound of a closing window.

Fairford: "Why did you say that, Lillian? You know it 's twenty minutes of five."

Mrs. Inglehart: "That 's a very charming girl, Jim — a Miss Roberta Lawrence. I want you to meet her. But perhaps you have met her already"—

Fairford: "No; but that is n't the point. Why did you say twenty minutes? I wish you had n't, dear!"

Mrs. Inglehart: "Well, it *is* twenty minutes — and more too; it 's twenty minutes of five. You said so yourself. Now don't tease, but go and prettify. That 's what *she* 's doing" — The sound of the lifting window is heard again, and then the voice of Miss Lawrence.

Miss Lawrence: "Mrs. Inglehart! Are you still there?"

Mrs. Inglehart, in a high key: "Yes!" In a low key to Fairford: "Now you must go! It 's a shame for you to stay here eavesdropping. And making me, too; and you so conscientious! 'Sh!"

Miss Lawrence: "I 'm in something of a dilemma. I don't know whether it had better be the green, or the blue."

Mrs. Inglehart: "Oh — the blue, dear; or no, the green — blue, I mean." In a low key to Fairford: "Now you have spoilt everything, and disgraced me before my guest. I can never forgive you!"

Fairford: "How have I done that?

She has said nothing that compromises either of you"—

Mrs. Inglehart: "You 've let her give herself away. You know that it 's for you she 's choosing between blue and green."

Fairford: "Bless my soul, how should I know such a thing?"

Mrs. Inglehart: "Don't you suppose I told her you were coming? And when she comes down and finds you here you won't be capable of seeming to have come just that instant."

Fairford: "If she asks"—

Mrs. Inglehart: "As if she would ask! She is too high-spirited, too noble-minded to go prying about; but it will kill her, all the same. You don't know how a girl like Roberta Lawrence, so frank herself, and so unsuspicious, will take such a thing. Of course, if it was I, I could laugh it off; but she will think that I did it purposely; she won't show it, but she will never believe that I was as innocent as she was in the matter."

Fairford: "It seems to me you 're not painting a very frank and unsuspicious character."

Mrs. Inglehart: "I mean I should in her place. You know what I mean. But if you prefer to vex me — She 'll be asking something else in another minute!"

Fairford: "But what do you want me to do?"

Mrs. Inglehart: "You must *think* what I want you to do. You have got me into this trouble, by your ridiculous promptness, and you must get me out."

Fairford: "Then let me go to my room, and I can't overhear anything more."

Mrs. Inglehart: "Oh, you think it 's so simple as that, do you? Wait a minute — I have it! You must go away! And you must come back in about ten minutes or so, as if you had n't been here at all. And you must apologize for being late; say you missed the train, or something like that, and" —

Fairford, sitting doggedly down: "No, I can't do anything of the kind."

Mrs. Inglehart: "You can't?"

Fairford: "Well, then, I won't. It would be acting a lie."

Mrs. Inglehart: "You accuse me of wishing you to lie."

Fairford: "I don't think you do it knowingly. But, Lillian, you must see" —

Mrs. Inglehart: "'Sh! There, she's putting up her window again!"

Miss Lawrence, from her window: "I've decided not to dress at him, Mrs. Inglehart. I am going to be perfectly passive, and let fate take its course. I'm going to wear my silver-gray."

Mrs. Inglehart: "Perfect!" In a low tone to Fairford, desperately: "It's too late for you to go away now. You might as well stay!"

Fairford: "But I don't understand. Why should Miss Lawrence dress at me? Have *you* dressed at me, Lillian?

You look heavenly in that — thing you 've got on ; I don't know what it is."

Mrs. Inglehart: " Oh, much pleasure your compliments give me, when I know what a cold, hollow heart they come from ! I may dress for you, but you won't gratify me in the smallest thing. Suppose your going away *does* have the appearance of deceit? Is a mere *appearance* so very killing, when it 's for such a good object? Oh, Jim! Do help me out! Think of the poor girl's feelings if she comes down and finds you here! She 'll *know* you overheard her. If you really cared for me" —

Fairford, rising with a groan, and gathering his bag up for going : " And if I go — if I do this against my reason and conscience, what shall you do with me when I come back?"

Mrs. Inglehart: "You 'll be so interested in Miss Lawrence you won't care."

Fairford: "That won't do, Lillian. I shall want my answer when I come back. Will you promise it?"

Mrs. Inglehart: "It 's very mean of you to make conditions! I 'll *listen* to you. But I won't even do that if you stay. And if you think I 'm asking you to act a lie, just think what a lie you 've been making *me* act."

Fairford: "I? How?"

Mrs. Inglehart: "By letting me see you before you saw her, when I promised mamma I would n't."

Fairford: "But why did you promise that? What" —

Mrs. Inglehart: "That has nothing to do with it. A promise is a promise, and sacred. Will you go? And when you come back, and find Miss Lawrence here, will you ask after me as if you had n't met me?"

Fairford: "No, certainly not. I can't carry the deceit as far as that."

Mrs. Inglehart: "Not to enable me to keep my promise? Very well, then, that shows that you don't trust me, and if you don't trust me, you can't care for me."

Fairford: "I don't trust you in the least, and I care all the world for you. For heaven's sake, Lillian, be candid with me, for once, and tell me what all this coil is! I know that whatever you 've got in your head, there 's nothing but truth in your heart, and if you would only be guided by that" —

Mrs. Inglehart, apparently fascinated by the idea: "Well, I will. I 'll tell you all about it. You see that we were talking about your coming, and I said to Roberta Lawrence — 'Sh! There 's her step! She 's coming out of her room — she 's on the stairs! Run, James, if you love me!" She pushes him towards the veranda steps, and without waiting to see him vanish round the corner of the house, she turns, and flies through the long window into the drawing-room, while Miss Lawrence emerges from the hallway, and Mrs. Wenham advances from the veranda on the side of the house opposite that which has just hidden Fairford from view.

IV

MISS LAWRENCE AND MRS. WENHAM

Miss Lawrence: "Mrs. Inglehart!" To Mrs. Wenham: "I thought Mrs. Inglehart was here!"

Mrs. Wenham: "And I thought I heard talking. But I must have dreamed it. I seem to have dozed over my book."

Miss Lawrence: "Perhaps you heard me calling down to her. I was consulting her about Mr. Fairford's taste in colors. Is n't he very late?" She looks in at the clock in the hall, and Mrs. Wenham looks in too.

An Indian Giver

Mrs. Wenham: "Yes; it 's nearly five, and he promised to be here at half past four. Something must have detained him; he 's usually so prompt."

Miss Lawrence, smiling: "Yes, terribly prompt, I believe. At least that 's the impression Mrs. Inglehart gives of him." The ladies have seated themselves, and Miss Lawrence, reclining in her chair, indifferently studies the effect of a ring on her left hand.

Mrs. Wenham, looking at her over her glasses: "You 've never met my nephew, I believe?"

Miss Lawrence: "No; and I 've no idea how he 'll like me. You know it 's very important he should like me. Mrs. Inglehart has given him to me."

Mrs. Wenham, dryly: "Yes, I have

been scolding Lillian for her nonsense. He is not hers to give."

Miss Lawrence: "Oh! To keep, then!"

Mrs. Wenham: "I am not so sure. Miss Lawrence, I know that you are a very frank person" —

Miss Lawrence: "Some people say merely brutal."

Mrs. Wenham: "No matter! I feel that I can speak frankly with you. Don't trust my daughter!"

Miss Lawrence: "This *is* frank."

Mrs. Wenham: "She acts upon impulses that she regrets. She is in love with James Fairford, I believe, and I know that he is in love with her. He was, before she married Mr. Inglehart, and I think she was with him;

but the affair never came to anything, because — because — It was Lillian's fault; she could n't be serious with him."

Miss Lawrence: "And now? Has he got over wanting her to be serious, or has she become so?"

Mrs. Wenham: "Lillian will never be serious — at least not like other people; and that is why I feel it my duty to be serious with you. No one knows Lillian as I do. If she saw that any one else wanted James, she would move heaven and earth to get him herself."

Miss Lawrence, laughing: "Really, what you say rather inclines me to try for him. I should like to see Mrs. Inglehart moving heaven and earth."

Mrs. Wenham: "Don't, my dear! I should simply leave the house. There is n't a thing she would n't do if she saw you wanted him." Miss Lawrence laughs more and more. "I know what nonsense she has been talking to you, and I made her promise, just to punish her, that she would let you meet him first, and have a chance to — I mean that she should be made to suffer a little for her wicked folly" —

Miss Lawrence: "Through some finesse of mine? Would n't that be rather too much theatre?"

Mrs. Wenham: "Yes, I don't know what she would n't do in her jealousy; for she 'd be frantically, blindly, madly jealous if she thought he cared for you the least bit."

An Indian Giver

Miss Lawrence: "Poor Mrs. Inglehart! I should like to see her jealous. It does n't seem in character. But I 'm greatly obliged to you for securing me the first innings. How do you propose to manage it?"

Mrs. Wenham: "That I shall leave entirely to Lillian. I suppose that as she 's out of the way, and he 's expected momentarily, she 's actually keeping her word, and" —

Miss Lawrence: "I 'm sitting here to intercept Mr. Fairford on his way into the house! Is n't it rather cold-blooded? But I don't mind! You don't think he could manage to escape me, somehow?"

Mrs. Wenham: "I shall be sitting here too; and I dare say Lillian has given directions where he 's to be received."

Miss Lawrence: "Heroic Mrs. Inglehart! I begin to quake a little. Do you know, if I had been *she*, I should have broken my word." After a thoughtful moment: "If one were really meditating an assault upon Mr. Fairford's affections, what should you say was his weakest side, Mrs. Wenham?"

Mrs. Wenham: "James?" Proudly: "He *has* no weak side."

Miss Lawrence: "Oh, I did n't say weak, I said *weakest.* Where is he least strong?"

Mrs. Wenham: "Except for his inconceivable folly in regard to Lillian, I should say that James Fairford was equally strong at all points. He is truth itself; promptitude, sincerity, justice, honor" —

Miss Lawrence, with a deep breath: "He *is* formidable."

Mrs. Wenham: "He despises anything like double-dealing, or prevarication, or even evasion. He will admire *you*, Miss Lawrence."

Miss Lawrence: "Oh, thank you! I begin to have my doubts." Mrs. Inglehart appears at one of the long veranda windows, and looks through them, with her hands lifted to either side of the casement. "Oh, come out, Mrs. Inglehart!"

V

MRS. INGLEHART, MISS LAWRENCE, MRS. WENHAM

Mrs. Inglehart: "It 's very tempting. But I can't, and I've got to take my mother away too, and consult about some little changes in receiving Mr. Fairford. You must keep him here until I come."

Miss Lawrence: "I wish he were here now. If he could only see you there as you 're standing now! I wish you could see yourself, and you 'd agree with me that there was never anything *quite* so graceful as that pose of yours."

Mrs. Inglehart: "You must tell him about it when he does come; that will be such a nice pose for *you*."

Miss Lawrence, rising and bobbing a courtesy to Mrs. Inglehart in acknowledgment of her little dig: "Thank you, *so* much!" To Mrs. Wenham, who joins her daughter: "And you 're actually going to leave me alone with Mr. Fairford!"

Mrs. Wenham: "You 'll be in the best of hands, my dear. Remember what I told you."

Miss Lawrence: "I shan't forget such a charge as that!"

Mrs. Inglehart: "A conspiracy?" She looks from one to the other; then over her shoulder, as she vanishes within: "Be sure to keep him; tell him he can't go to his room just yet."

Miss Lawrence, calling after her: "Oh, I 'll *keep* him." When Mrs.

Inglehart and her mother are out of sight, she bows herself forward in silent laughter, and when she lifts her face out of her hands again, she confronts Fairford, who is stealthily mounting the veranda steps, with a manner the reverse of his earlier brusqueness and severity. At sight of him Miss Lawrence springs to her feet, and comes gayly toward him with outstretched hand: "Mr. Fairford? Miss Lawrence! Mrs. Inglehart has commissioned me to welcome you in her place, and to keep you here, while she and Mrs. Wenham are taking counsel together about your room. Won't you sit down till they come?"

VI

FAIRFORD AND MISS LAWRENCE.

Fairford, backing upon a chair, with his bag in his hand and his overcoat on his arm: "Thank you." He falls into the chair and stares helplessly at her.

Miss Lawrence: "Was your train late, or did you take a later one? You see the fame of your promptness has preceded you, and you were expected at half past four."

Fairford: "The train was n't late; I 'm late — I 've been walking" —

Miss Lawrence, politely: "From the station!"

Fairford, with a deep sigh of relief: "Yes — I walked — from the station, yes."

Miss Lawrence: "Then that accounts for it. And it must take some time for the wayfarer who is n't personally conducted to find his way round to the entrance of Mrs. Inglehart's house. A house naturally fronts before, but if it has the sea in the rear, there 's a certain temptation to front behind, and Mrs. Inglehart's house has yielded to the temptation. Don't you think it 's like her? So full of—unexpectedness!"

Fairford: "Yes; very singular. Very puzzling—if you 've never been here before."

Miss Lawrence, keenly: "And is this the first time you 've been here?"

Fairford: "I"—Desperately: "I've never been here before to-day."

Miss Lawrence: "Do you mean,

never before to-day, or never to-day before?"

Fairford: "I mean, never before to-day; not to-day before."

Miss Lawrence: "Then there *is* a difference! I'm so glad; I thought there was n't when I asked." She muses aloud: "Let me see! He has never been here before to-day; but he may have been here to-day before. Is that sense? Let me try it the other way! He has been here to-day before, but he has never been here before to-day." Fairford gazes uneasily at her. "I can't make it out; but I'll ask Mrs. Inglehart when she comes; she'll know. I'll put it as a conundrum: If a gentleman has never been here before to-day, and yet has been here to-day before, when has the gentleman been here before?" Fairford listens with signs of increasing terror, which culminate in a violent start when she turns suddenly upon him: "Mr. Fairford, I 'm tempted to make you a confidence! Oh — ha, ha, ha! Don't be frightened. It 's only something psychical. But I have had such a strange impression in regard to you."

Fairford, in alarm: "Me?"

Miss Lawrence: "Yes. I wonder if I may venture to speak of it; but with your frankness — oh, all your virtues have anticipated you; every one was here promptly at half past four! — I 'm sure you 'll answer me. As you came up the veranda steps, just now, I had that weird sense of its all having happened before. You have had it: every one has; but at this instant it's so vivid with me that it seems as if you must *share* it with me." Laughingly: "Do you have a been-here-before feeling too?"

Fairford: "I can't say — I — May I ask what you mean?"

Miss Lawrence: "I don't wonder you're surprised. But I'm so curious to know whether two persons could have that weird seizure at the same moment in regard to the same thing. Of course it's impossible, and I ought really to beg your pardon, but as you came up the veranda steps, just now, it flashed upon me, 'He feels as if he had been here before.' Perhaps it was a strange look — Excuse me; I'm odiously personal. Will you please to make a remark?"

Fairford: "I! A remark?"

Miss Lawrence: "Yes; anything—anything to turn the conversation. I've made all the remarks up to this point. I see you don't like psychical confidences."

Fairford: "Yes—I like them very much. But I wish to say—I ought to tell you—I don't know how to"—He stops and stares at her.

Miss Lawrence, looking down at her dress on either side of her, and twitching it: "Is there something on my gown? A bug? A caterpillar? No?" Laughing: "A woman always thinks something 's wrong with her dress when people stare. But perhaps it 's only the color? It 's a very peculiar shade of gray; I 've been told by flatterers that I look like a wraith in it, and you look — excuse me, really, Mr. Fairford! you look as if I *did* look like a wraith!"

Fairford: "Not at all, I assure you. But I — but in regard to your psychical experience, I wish — I feel bound to say" —

Miss Lawrence: "Then you like that kind of thing! Do let me tell you another! It 's apropos of this gown, which I wish you to notice particularly, so that you can corroborate me when I tell Mrs. Inglehart." She rises, and puts it in evidence by slowly turning in front of her chair; Fairford starts up, and backs away in vague alarm. "Should you have thought I put it on for you?"

Fairford, gasping: " For me ? "

Miss Lawrence: " No ? Did n't you know it ? " She fixes him with a piercing glance, and then sinks into her chair again, laughing, while he remains standing, aghast. " It can't be the first time that you 've been dressed at by a young lady; it 's something that 's always happening when men are expected in houses where girls are. Don't you know that ? "

Fairford, with relief: " I suppose — I dare say " —

Miss Lawrence: " But, *unless you know*, you never could imagine the rest of what I 'm going to tell you. I 've just had the most awful scare. A little while before you came, I was up in my room, which looks out over the roof of the veranda here, and I fell into a hopeless doubt between blue and green. Which should I wear? I could n't decide, and as I had left Mrs. Inglehart sitting here alone, I indulged myself in a little impulse. I put up my window, and asked Mrs. Inglehart which it should be, and then after I had decided, I decided over again, and put up my window to tell her so. It was this last time that I had my fright. I thought — I fancied — I dreamed — that I heard another voice just before I spoke, and that this voice was a man's voice. Of course it was impossible, in the nature of things, even if it was so, but it served, for the time being. As soon as I could I reasoned myself out of it. Mrs. Inglehart could n't be so ungenerous — so unkind — as to let me suppose she was here alone, and even if she could, the man would have insisted upon giving me some proof of his presence, if he was a gentleman. Of course if it were the groom, or the gardener, or some workman about the place, I need n't care; and so, as I said, I reasoned myself out of it. But it was a very pretty scare while it lasted, I can assure you. I really suppose it was this that gave me that been-here-before feeling when I saw you coming up the steps. Ah, here comes Mrs. Inglehart, and I'm off duty; but please don't speak to her of it, will you? I wish to tell her later myself. You promise?"

Fairford: "Yes" —

Miss Lawrence: "Oh, thank you.

I'll be back directly, Lilly. I 've kept Mr. Fairford safely for you." She waves her hand to Mrs. Inglehart as she appears at the parlor window, and vanishes through the door into the hall.

VII

MRS. INGLEHART AND FAIRFORD

Mrs. Inglehart, coming out on the veranda: "What is it you are not to tell me?"

Fairford: "Who is that, Lillian?"

Mrs. Inglehart: "It 's Miss Lawrence, of course. Don't you like her?"

Fairford: "Against my reason and conscience, I consented to go away and come back, in this disgraceful fashion, to spare your feelings, and hers; and the result is that I shall do neither, and that I shall not be able to hold up my head."

Mrs. Inglehart: "Why, what in the world has happened?"

Fairford: "That is what I can't tell you; that 's what I promised I would n't tell. You can ask Miss Lawrence; I am going away."

Mrs. Inglehart: "Going away!"

Fairford: "I have been placed in a thoroughly false position. To oblige you, I have consented to act a falsehood, and I have done it so badly that"—

Mrs. Inglehart: "Of course you 've done it badly. I expected that. But what of it? Did she get it out of you?"

Fairford: "I must leave you to learn from Miss Lawrence what has passed.

I have given my word, and I must keep it. Good-by!" He bows coldly, and goes toward the veranda steps.

Mrs. Inglehart, running to intercept him: "But you are not actually going! You can't be so insane, so wicked as that!"

Fairford: "You 've made it impossible for me to stay. The truth must come out, and then you will see why."

Mrs. Inglehart: "But no matter how bad the truth is, you 'll only make it worse by going!"

Fairford: "I must be judge of that. Will you please let me pass?"

Mrs. Inglehart: "Do you think this is treating me very nicely? What shall I say to Miss Lawrence? How shall I explain? Oh, Jim, dear! Don't be boyish! I've no doubt that as soon as I know what the trouble is, I can make it right. I might have known she would tangle you up, somehow; but it can't be bad enough to drive you from my house. Think how it will look!"

Fairford: "I must leave appearances to you, hereafter; you can manage them better."

Mrs. Inglehart: "Is that what *she* said of me?"

Fairford: "Lillian!"

Mrs. Inglehart: "I did n't mean that, Jim; indeed I did n't. But you can't imagine how awkward it will be for me if you go; what a false position it will place *me* in. Don't be selfish! Don't go. *I ask you to stay.*" She looks at him significantly.

Fairford: "It's too late. I'd have given the world to hear that from you a little while ago; but now" — He falters.

Mrs. Inglehart: "Very well; go, then! *I* know what the trouble is. She knew that you had been here before, and she could only have done it by eavesdropping."

Fairford: "No, Lillian; it was we who were eavesdropping."

Mrs. Inglehart: "Then it's not eavesdropping to listen from a window, but it is from a veranda? She heard every word we were saying here, and her calling down to me was a mere ruse. I might have known it at the time. But of course, if you think I was capable of eavesdropping and she was n't, that settles the matter, and I have no more to say. Don't let me keep you, Mr. Fairford." She suddenly bursts into tears, and catching her handkerchief to her face, flies through the window and vanishes, at the same moment that Mrs. Wenham appears at the hallway door.

VIII

MRS. WENHAM AND FAIRFORD

Mrs. Wenham, coming forward to where Fairford remains standing motionless, bag in hand: "Why, James! You 've got here at last. What in the world kept you? Have you just come?"

Fairford: "I 'm just going."

Mrs. Wenham: "Going? Without seeing Lillian?"

Fairford: "I have seen her, and — that's why I'm going."

Mrs. Wenham: "She is n't sending you away!"

Fairford: "No, no! Not in that sense of the word. We've quarreled. Aunt Harriet, I wish to tell you" —

Mrs. Wenham: "Oh, you need n't tell me! I know what it is. It's part of that miserable nonsense of hers about — But you have n't *seen* Miss Lawrence!"

Fairford, in dull despair: "Yes, I've seen Miss Lawrence."

Mrs. Wenham: "And Lillian was angry with you on that account, and in her ridiculous jealousy — Well, then, I'm glad she's lost you, James."

Fairford: "I'm not, Aunt Harriet.

And I 'm afraid it is n't just as you think it is. I must tell you something — I promised not to tell Lillian, but I may tell you" —

Mrs. Wenham: "You may tell *me* *any*thing, James. Whom did you promise?"

Fairford: "Miss Lawrence. I came at half past four as I promised, and I found Lillian on the veranda here" —

Mrs. Wenham: "Lillian? And where was Miss Lawrence?"

Fairford: "I don't know — or I did n't then; but it seems somewhere overhead; and presently, while we were talking, she put up her window, and began calling down to Lillian, and asking her what she should wear. Lillian seemed to have forgotten about her" —

Mrs. Wenham: "Wretched child!"

Fairford: "And when she remembered, she said she had promised you Miss Lawrence should see me first, and I must go away, and come back so as to give the impression that I had n't been here."

Mrs. Wenham: "But you never consented to such an outrageous imposition?"

Fairford: "I did n't like it; but I thought Lillian was right in thinking Miss Lawrence would be annoyed if she knew that I had overheard her, and I consented — in violation of every principle of my life. When I came back, Miss Lawrence was here."

Mrs. Wenham: "Well?"

Fairford: "It was useless. She

began to let me understand at once that she knew I had been here already, and — in short, the game was up. She kept the whole thing in such form that I could neither admit it nor deny it. When Lillian returned and Miss Lawrence left us, I threatened to go away, and she begged me to stay, and after we had some hot words, she told me to go, and — here I am. What is it all about, Aunt Harriet? Why should she promise you to let Miss Lawrence receive me, and why should Miss Lawrence wish to dress especially to please me?"

Mrs. Wenham: "I will tell you, James. But first sit down and put that bag somewhere. You 're not going, and Lillian never meant you to go, any more than you meant to leave her when you threatened it. I'm glad I know just how the case stands, and I think I can make you see Lillian's behavior in the right light, though I am thoroughly ashamed of it myself, and disgusted with her, and I've told her so. You will always have to account for something that is wholly incomprehensible in Lillian, if you expect to understand her at all."

Fairford, patiently: "Yes, that is what I have always tried to do."

Mrs. Wenham: "Well, then, you can easily imagine that when she had consented to your coming here to-day on terms that any one else would feel were the same as accepting you, she should feel the need of putting it out of her power to accept you — or rather that she would have to be in the greatest danger of losing you — before she was able to accept you."

Fairford, making an effort: "I think I can conceive of something like that. What has it to do with Miss Lawrence's trying to please my taste in dress?"

Mrs. Wenham: "Simply this. Before she could realize your loss, Lillian had to give you to some one else."

Fairford, after a moment's reflection: "If you wanted anything, would you put it out of your power, in order to realize your desire for it?"

Mrs. Wenham: "No, but Lillian would; and I should respect you a great deal more if you renounced her forever, and took a fancy to Miss Lawrence. But I hope you won't, for I know that Lillian is devotedly fond of you."

Fairford: "I 'm afraid there 's no danger of my renouncing her. Whom did she give me to?"

Mrs. Wenham: "Oh, you poor, single-minded man! To Miss Lawrence."

Fairford: "And did Miss Lawrence know it?"

Mrs. Wenham: "James, I don't wonder Lillian finds you rather trying at times. Of course she knew it! And I insisted upon her being allowed to meet you first, and to — to — to" —

Fairford: "What?"

Mrs. Wenham: "My dear, you are enough to try the patience of a saint.

Such innocence as yours is *criminal!*"
At this word, Mrs. Inglehart suddenly emerges from the drawing-room window upon the veranda.

IX

MRS. INGLEHART, MRS. WENHAM, AND FAIRFORD

Mrs. Inglehart: "I will not have you abusing me to James, mother."

Mrs. Wenham: "I was not speaking of you!"

Mrs. Inglehart: "You said criminal."

Mrs. Wenham: "I said James was criminal — for being so good."

Mrs. Inglehart: "Oh! And what have you been saying about me?"

Mrs. Wenham: "I 've been explaining you."

Mrs. Inglehart: "Very well, then, I won't *be* explained — above all to Mr. Fairford." She sits down and looks at her mother. "I thought he was going."

Fairford, appealingly: "You know I could n't go, Lillian" —

Mrs. Inglehart, ignoring him: "He *said* he was going; but perhaps that was a man's way of meaning that he was n't. You never can tell what they mean from what they say. Do you know where Miss Lawrence is, mother? I wish to tell her that Mr. Fairford has changed his mind, and is going to stay after all. She may not like to come to dinner in that case; or Mr. Fairford may not like to meet her. They seem both to be victims of the same deceit, poor dears. I 'm sure I don't know who has tried to deceive them, except for their own good."

Fairford: "I never doubted your motive, Lillian. I know how generous you are. I only objected to the false position that I was placed in with reference to Miss Lawrence."

Mrs. Inglehart, always ignoring him: "I hope you are satisfied, mother, with having insisted on my letting Miss Lawrence meet Mr. Fairford first, instead of receiving him myself as a hostess should."

Mrs. Wenham, rising in virtuous indignation: "Lillian, I will not allow you to be so perverse! I don't care *how* old you are. You are acting like a naughty child, but I suppose it 's because you 're thoroughly ashamed of yourself. I 've told James all about your wicked folly, and if I were he I should go away, and leave you to get out of it as you could. I wash my hands of the whole affair." Mrs. Wenham sweeps indoors and abandons the cousins to their own devices.

X

MRS. INGLEHART AND FAIRFORD

Mrs. Inglehart, after a marked silence, very mildly and meekly: "Well, Jim!"

Fairford: "Well, Lil!"

Mrs. Inglehart: "What do you think of me now?"

Fairford: "I have n't changed my mind; but I *think* I understand you a little better than I did."

Mrs. Inglehart: "And you still blame me? Remember I don't know what my mother 's been saying about me."

Fairford: "Nothing that does n't make you dearer to me. I think she was too hard upon you for a harmless joke like that."

Mrs. Inglehart: "Oh, Jim, how sweet you are! Do you really mean it?"

Fairford: "I wish you would let me prove it. I wish you could let me employ my life in proving it."

Mrs. Inglehart: "Oh, you know I always trusted you. You 're truth itself!"

Fairford: "And I always trusted you, though" —

Mrs. Inglehart: "Though I 'm not truth itself."

Fairford: "Something like that."

Mrs. Inglehart: "How delicious! You know I always did think your candor was delicious." She puts up her hands to the back of her head, and tries to look round at the top of her chair. "I seem to be caught" —

Fairford: "Can I help you?"

Mrs. Inglehart: "Oh, no." But he comes to her and frees the knot of her hair from a loose fibre of the cane which has caught it. "Thank you so much, James." He does not go away, and he does not relinquish the hand she had put up to help free her hair. He sits down on the arm of her chair, and scrutinizes her left-hand fingers critically.

Mrs. Inglehart: "Well?"

Fairford: "I thought I could n't be mistaken in the size. May I try it on?"

Mrs. Inglehart: "Why, if you 've taken all the trouble to bring it" —

Fairford: "I ventured to do it."

Mrs. Inglehart, looking fondly up into his eyes while he fits the ring on her finger: "It was no great risk."

Fairford: "Does it hurt? Is it too tight?"

Mrs. Inglehart: "It is too tight, but it does n't — hurt!" A sound of quick footfalls and rustling skirts makes itself heard within the drawing-room. Mrs. Inglehart jumps to her feet. "Oh, good gracious! There 's that detestable girl! I forgot all about her again! Run, Jim! Or no, it 's too late now. Stay!" The sound of the quick footfalls and the rustling skirts within grows vaguer. "Yes, go now. She 's executing a little manœuvre. She 's seen us, but she 's pretending she did n't, and she 's gone back to give us time before she comes out through the hall door. That 's all right. Run along now, dear, and leave me to manage with her. I don't think she 'll get anything out of *me* that I don't want her to know. Why don't you go, James? Oh! *Goose!*" She puts her arms round his neck, as he bends over her, and kisses him, and then pushes him decisively away. As he disappears round the corner of the veranda, she calls: "Miss Lawrence! Roberta! Is that you?"

Miss Lawrence, within: "I am looking for a handkerchief I left — Oh, here it is!" She appears at the door, and looks out. "I thought Mr. Fairford" —

Mrs. Inglehart: "He was here a moment ago, but he 's gone to his room — I suppose to his room. I 've been so much interested in your psychological experience, Roberta."

Miss Lawrence: "Then he 's told! I might have expected it."

Mrs. Inglehart: "You 'd have been disappointed if you had. Men need n't tell things. They 've merely to say they won't, and then women are inspired with the facts. I guessed what had happened as soon as I saw the kind of trouble he was in, and I envied you the opportunity you had of — rattling him. Do tell me just how you did it."

Miss Lawrence: "Do you think that will be necessary?"

Mrs. Inglehart: "No, I don't know that I do. And I admire you for your reticence. I supposed frankness was your strong point."

Miss Lawrence: "Is n't that always a forlorn hope with us? The pose of utter despair? The last resort?"

Mrs. Inglehart: "Perhaps it is. I was just going to try it with you. There seems nothing else for it."

Miss Lawrence: "Ah, you pique my curiosity. What is it you *could* be frank about? I mean" —

Mrs. Inglehart: "I see what you mean. But you remember that a little while ago, here, I gave you James Fairford?"

Miss Lawrence: "Yes; and 'the gods themselves cannot resume their gifts.'"

Mrs. Inglehart: "I don't know about the gods, but I 'm sure the goddesses could. My dear Roberta, I want him back. I must have him. Come, now, be very, very nice, and let me have him again! Won't you? I know that legally, and everything else, he belongs to you, and I suppose that in a court of justice I should n't have the slightest chance. But I throw myself on your mercy. See!" She comes over to where the girl has seated herself, and drops on her knees before her. "Let me have him, dear! I'd no idea I cared anything about him till I'd parted with him. Come! Say the word!"

Miss Lawrence: "And I, what am I to do with the wealth of affection that I had prepared to lavish upon him?"

Mrs. Inglehart: "Oh, give it to somebody else! Jim won't mind."

Miss Lawrence: "Ah, that's just what I'm not so sure about! I've an idea that he is madly devoted to me. In fact, I can't give him up till I know from his own lips that he wishes to be given up. Yes, he must renounce me"—

Mrs. Inglehart: "Oh, but I assure

you he does n't care anything about you" —

Miss Lawrence: "That I must know from himself. I insist upon his choosing between us!"

Mrs. Inglehart, rising: "Do you really mean it?"

Miss Lawrence: "Yes; I think it would be fun."

Mrs. Inglehart, with genuine feeling: "I can't say it's my idea of a joke. Well, then, it may be very inhospitable, and all that, and I wish it could have come about a little more gracefully, but I have to tell you — Oh, have you hurt yourself?" She takes note of the handkerchief which Miss Lawrence has wrapped around her left hand; the girl puts the hand behind her. "Can't I give you something? Arnica? Pond's extract? How did you do it? *Putting up the window?*"

Miss Lawrence, in embarrassment: "No, no" —

Mrs. Inglehart, dryly: "I 'm very sorry. Those window-catches are awkward things. I 've caught my fingers when I 've been thinking of something else."

Miss Lawrence: "It was n't the window-catch, I assure you, Mrs. Inglehart, and I don't know how to tell you what it is, exactly. I thought it would be so simple; but — I ought never to have let you give me Mr. Fairford."

Mrs. Inglehart: "Oh, don't mind that. I 've taken him back again."

Miss Lawrence: "Oh, that does n't make it right on my part. I meant to have told you before; but I could n't get the chance; and then it seemed to get more and more complicated, and" —

Mrs. Inglehart, impatiently: "Well?"

Miss Lawrence: "Well!" She puts out her left hand to Mrs. Inglehart, and covers her eyes with the handkerchief she has caught from it.

Mrs. Inglehart, clutching it wildly: "An engagement ring!"

Miss Lawrence: "Yes, we were engaged last week, and when you began to speak to me, and I did n't know quite how — I had n't the courage" —

Mrs. Inglehart, flinging Miss Lawrence's hand from her: "Then it was all a trick from the beginning! And you let me make a fool of myself in that way, and all the time you were engaged! And you said you never met him before" —

Miss Lawrence, in amaze: "How could I say such a thing? We 've known each other for years."

Mrs. Inglehart: "So it appears. And I don't know how you could say you 'd never seen him, but I know you did say it. Perhaps you 'd like *two* engagement rings. You may have mine" — She tries to get it off.

Miss Lawrence: "What *do* you mean? What are you doing? Whom are you talking about?"

Mrs. Inglehart, still struggling violently with the ring: "James Fairford. You may have both his rings" —

Miss Lawrence: "James Fairford! I don't want his rings — either of them. I 'm engaged to Arthur Wayland! Do you think there 's only one man in the world?"

Mrs. Inglehart, after a moment's daze: "Then you — you — I see — yes! Oh, you dear! Oh, I 'm so happy for you!" She falls upon Miss Lawrence's neck and clasps her to her heart. "Arthur Wayland? He 's charming, and he 's a very lucky fellow, but he deserves you if any one does. Ah, ha, ha! Oh, hu, hu, hu!" Mrs. Wenham appears at one corner of the veranda, and Fairford at the other, from different sides of the house.

An Indian Giver

XI

MRS. WENHAM, FAIRFORD, MISS LAWRENCE, MRS. INGLEHART

Mrs. Wenham, sternly: "What is the matter, Lillian?"

Mrs. Inglehart, between tears and laughter: "Nothing, nothing! Roberta is engaged, and I'm merely congratulating her."

The Riverside Press
Electrotyped and printed by H. O. Houghton & Co.
Cambridge, Mass, U. S. A.